To Scorch a Quartz Thorn

Fleur DeVillainy

Introduction and Trigger warnings

To Scorch a Quartz Thorn is a new adult romantic fantasy intended for individuals 18+ years old and may not be suitable for all ages.

This book includes the following trigger warnings: open door sexual activity, blood, and mild profanity

CHAPTER ONE

Evie

"Did you hear?" Charlotte whispers, and I jump in my seat, pricking my finger with my needle. A drop of blood falls and stains the cream square of cloth I was failing miserably to embroider.

"Drat," I grumble under my breath as I look up at the other three ladies Queen Rose appointed to tour this summer with her. It has already been a month since I left the manor to join the queen at Verdigris Falls. The thought of traveling and spending time on the coast filled me with excitement at first, but after weeks of relentless gossiping, embroidery, and tea, I now missed the peace and quiet of the stables with my horses and my dogs.

Annalise glances toward the queen, then leans over me, whispering to Charlotte. "Don't tell me you're talking about the scandal in this week's gossip paper the servants brought from town! I couldn't believe that Lord Elsem—"

"Don't ye have anything better to do than sit around and talk about who's marrying who or breaking off what engagement?" I set my needlework to the side with a sigh. At this point, I'd rather burn it.

"This could affect our future Evangeline," Charlotte humphs as she turns to Annalise. "They say he's turned down every eligible suitor and has sweet eyes for his maid! Can you believe it? A lord falling in love with his maid."

"I don't see what frivolously gossiping about someone ye hardly know could do for our future." I purse my lips in disapproval.

Turning my head to where the queen paints before the window, I let my gaze stray to the rolling hills of Heather and the glittering sea behind as the girls chitter on.

The prospect of marriage is not one I am particularly fond of, especially after my father, the duke, decided to take the matter in his own hands and sell me off like cattle.

Deep down, I always hoped there would be more for me out there. A silly fantasy I now realize, but one I had desperately clung to. I longed for adventure and the kind of love that doesn't spark only after it's been signed for on paper.

But come spring, I am to marry Lord Charles to strengthen our alliance with the kingdom of Caelo and there is nothing I can do to stop that. That is my duty as the only heir to my father, Lord Gramont's fortune.

"Evangeline. Evangeline!" Ellie hisses. I look down to see smoke has begun to curl in lazy spirals from my palms.

"Oh!" I exclaim, rubbing my hands together as a blush creeps into my cheeks. "I'm so sorry." I look wide eyed toward the girls, who grin back at me.

"What's on your mind, dear?" Charlotte says as she cocks her head to the side.

"Apologies, I was daydreaming and didn't mean to lose control of my powers." My gaze drops to my hands clenched tightly in my lap.

"Powers not utilized and practiced are wasted," Queen Rose says matter-of-factly as she sets down her paintbrush and gestures to one of the servants before settling in a recliner. "Bring us tea."

"But, Your Majesty, as ladies of the court, should we not focus on more important matters?" Ellie asks.

The queen raises an eyebrow and looks at each of us in turn before steepling her fingers together. "Show me."

"Yer Majesty, uh..." I stutter, reaching for my embroidery as the other ladies scramble for their past times.

"No, not your frivolous tasks." Queen Rose waves dismissively toward us. "Show me your powers. I did not pick the four of you merely because you were the daughters of royals."

Her statement shocks me and I turn toward her. "But, Yer Majesty…"

"No buts. Come now, all of you. Charlotte, being so close to the sea you should have no trouble. Show me."

"Yes, Your Majesty." Charlotte stands and curtsies before holding her hands out. The room fills with the smell of rain, and out of thin air, she conjures an orb of water slowly growing and orbiting between her palms. With a flick of her wrist, she lifts the orb into the air and it shatters, cascading into a fine mist. The queen nods in approval. She raises her hand and a breeze pushes open the windows to whisk the humidity away.

"Very good. Annalise?" Annalise stands and the air crackles. Small bolts of lightning flicker along her fingertips and up her wrists. My hair stands on end, lifting away from my face as she moves her arms gracefully. Her whole body glows ethereally until she reels the magic back into herself.

"Fabulous." The queen claps her hands, then turns to face Ellie and I.

"I'll go first." Ellie pushes to her feet. She rubs her hands together and closes her eyes.

I wait expectantly, the ticking of the clock on the mantle continuing its endless pace. My palms begin to sweat as I watch her sway side to side but nothing seems to change.

"It's alright, Ellie, another time." Queen Rose starts.

"No!" Ellie's eyes fly open, her normal green irises replaced by rings of smoke. Shadows radiate off her body in waves until the five of us are cast in complete and utter darkness. I jump up when I hear someone squeal in fear and tentatively try to reach for Ellie.

"Ellie... You can stt..top...now," Charlotte whispers, but the darkness only grows more dense. I hear the sound of porcelain shattering on the floor as the women around me try to escape.

Steadying myself, I take a deep breath and reach deep inside, calling forth my powers. A small spark stretches and grows from my palm until it becomes a living butterfly. It launches itself above my head, casting a dim glow before me.

"Come on, Evie, you can do this," I whisper to myself as I slowly pull on the thread of power until a second and third butterfly appear. They take flight as I continue to conjure more flames until the darkness slowly abides. They flutter above us, winking out of existence one by one; I keep my eyes trained above us until the very last one fades.

I rush toward Ellie, her eyes still clouded in shadows.

"Ellie, can ye hear me?" I snap my fingers in front of her but her expression stays lost.

The girls gather around us, worry etched on their faces.

"Ellie?" I ask again, taking her ice cold hand in mine. Without a second thought, I send a heat wave through her, hoping it'll break the spell she's under.

"Ow!" She instantly withdraws her hand from mine. Her eyes are once again clear. "What was that?" Ellie exclaims, massaging her palm.

"We could ask ye the same thing," I say in a long exhale and straighten my skirt.

"Evangeline, that was amazing," Annalise whispers.

I turn toward them and take in the ladies' shocked faces and then the queen's, who smiles at me like a cat with the cream.

CHAPTER TWO

Gavin

"Bloody fucking storms," I mumble as I scan the list of supplies my first mate handed to me. "What do you mean? It's going to take at least a month for the repairs."

"Captain, the main mast is down, half the sails are ripped beyond repair, there are leaks–" I hold my hand up.

"You're right, Rowan, I'm sorry. I was hoping the damages were not this severe." The storm—abnormally turbulent this early in summer, had caught us by surprise. I rake a hand through my auburn hair. Fuck. There is only one option left..

"I bloody hate having to dally in port," I whisper to myself. If the weather is on our side, we might be able to get the repairs done in a month's time.

An entire month on shore.

I pinch my nose in exasperation. "Tell me the cargo made it safely, at least."

The last thing I need is to know that the cargo we spent the last three months collecting is at the bottom of the sea... together with the rum.

"Every last crate is intact and accounted for," she says, sliding another detailed list on my ebony desk but averting her eyes. Her fingers drum restlessly against the wood.

"But?" I lift an eyebrow.

Rowan sighs, and her green eyes finally meet mine. "Well, Pepper chewed up your favorite pair of leather boots during the storm—"

"Bloody seven seas." I roll my eyes.

Rowan is already rushing to his defense, arms out to the sides and palms open. "I'm sure he was nervous! You know how much of a big baby he is!"

Huffing, I look down at the massive three-headed mastiff at my feet. He whines and puts his wrinkled faces between his paws, his tail beating the wooden floor.

"I suppose I was bound to be forced off this ship one way or another." I pull a leather pouch from the drawer and toss it at my first mate. "Make sure you restock the larder. I don't plan on touching land again for quite some time after this stop."

"Aye, aye Captain." She slips the pouch into her pocket, the coins clanking merrily, and leaves the room. I know she's going to find us the best deals, just as I know a few of those coppers will find themselves in the hands of orphaned children because she was one of them once.

"Come on, you brute," I say to Pepper. "If I have to face this land-loving town, you have to come with me." The mastiff bounds to his feet, tongue lolling as I strap on my daggers and tie my hair with a leather throng at the base of my neck.

"Where are you off to, Captain?" Two voices call. I stare up at the rigging to see the twins, Gulliver and Oliver, hanging from the rigging, unhooking one of the torn sails.

"Town," I shout up. "Be careful you don't fall and break your necks. I already have Pepper here to keep an eye on."

"Yes, Captain." They shout in unison as they unhook the last knot. The torn sail falls, hitting the deck with a loud thump that vibrates the wood beneath my feet.

"Gulliver! Oliver!" Rowan's harsh voice rumbles from behind me. "I told you to unhook and lower the torn sail, not let it drop like a floppy fish." I turn to see her shaking her head. "Captain, if you pick up any more strays on our journey—"

I raise an eyebrow before casting my eyes back up to the boys sheepishly racing each other down the rigging. "Don't forget, you were once one of those strays."

"I'd suggest you improve your recruitment skills, then. How about a couple of misfits that don't have a death wish, perhaps? That don't make it their mission to rip this bloody ship apart, hey!

Gulliver, for the seven seas, *be careful!*" Panic is rising in Rowan's voice as the boy has only one leg hooked on the rigging. He reminds me of the monkeys I had seen in the Elguco jungle on the other side of the planet.

"Ma'm it's fine, let us work!" the boy responds and sends a flying kiss in Rowan's direction, making my first officer shake her head in exasperation.. "I'll feed him to the sharks if he calls me Ma'm again." I suppress a smile at Rowans' concern hidden under her usual stoic exterior. She lifts her hand to her eyes to shade them from the sun and have a better look at the boys. "We should have taken that basilisk egg from the black market and left these reckless beasties there instead," she lies in a whisper.

I cross my arms over my chest and watch the twins, nearly identical save for the deep scar that ran from Gulliver's right temple, down to his cheek. What Rowan often forgets is that these boys, and most of my crew, don't have a death wish because they have already bartered with death once. Some of them, such as the boys, had experienced unspeakable things but they had all eagerly reached for my hand when I had tended it to them. We were walking through the black market in Asthroth, cove of the pirates, when the boys were being sold as slaves; they were only six. At the sight of these kids, with tattered clothes and dirt smeared all over their faces and bare feet, Pepper *accidentally* knocked the slave trader down as he was cutting Gulliver's face. Punishment for protecting his brother. I still remember the fire in Gulliver's eyes; it was the look of someone who, despite the young age, had looked death in the face and told him to piss off.

I sigh, running a hand through my hair. They had worked hard, had learned to be respectful, and were worth every gold coin I had handed over for their freedom. "These two are not nearly as reckless as Chef was when we first found him on the Cyprian islands," I chuckle, reminiscing about Chef's quick temper that used to cause all sorts of brawls on shore. "That was one hell of a trip. The tradesman wanted you to sell nareau silk in exchange for their hallucinogenic spice; I would have done anything to see the look on the merchant's face when the silk disintegrated as we pulled away from the dock. With a stow-a-way, nonetheless."

"To be fair, we didn't know he had given us a phony product. Plus, we fetched a great price for that spice and the best cook to boot."

Oliver and Gulliver still dangle like little monkeys, making Rowan catch her breath everytime they fake a fall. Rowan sighs. "If you need me, I'll be under deck. My heart can't take watching these two idiots work." She glances up once more and moves to the stairs.

I shield my eyes as me and Pepper make our way down the gangplank, seagulls wheeling and crying above us, and I mentally prepare for all the googling citizens. Three headed dogs were not unheard of but they were rare this north of the continent. I had bartered for him as a pup years ago on another trip to Asthroth to trade Shadowvale's prized amethysts for rare southern pigment. I hated traveling to the pirate ridden town, it was chaotic, lawless and dangerous, but it also had diamonds in its rough, and having one of the most reckless crews at sea also meant that, unlike most ships, we had no problem docking amongst pirates and doing business.

By contrast, the streets by the port of Verdigris Falls burst with a vibrant energy. Dock workers unload crates of goods from ships. Sailors, with their sun-kissed faces and weather-worn clothes, make their way to the closest tavern. There are merchants, locals, and even some ladies strolling about, eager to catch a glimpse of the exotic treasures brought back from distant shores. I already missed the sound of the waves crashing against my ship.

Pepper barks, tugging at his leash as the smell of roasted meat and stale ale reaches us when we pass Othello's Wood.

"Fine, but we will not linger longer than we need to sate ourselves." He cocks his heads at me, then trots beside me, cheerfully wagging his tail as I push open the tavern door. We take a seat in the back corner near the bar and I lean back, watching the room. Groups of sailors clump around tables, eating plates of roasted meat and swinging down chilled pints of local ale. The barmaid leans over the bar, refilling mugs.

"Darla, did you hear the queen is hosting a ball in a week's time?" A male with a mop of curly auburn hair says as he leans back in his chair, admiring her.

"There has been nothing but talk about the ball ever since she came into town for her summer stay. I hear there is a handsome duke from a neighboring kingdom coming to visit." She bats her eyelashes at him.

He scoffs, pushing forward in his seat until he's nearly nose to nose with her before spinning a silver coin between his fingers.

"What good is a duke who's betrothed to one of the queen's ladies to you, when you could have me?" He winks before slipping it between her bosom.

"What is someone like *you* doing here?" a male slurs as he slams his fists on my table, his other hand sloshing beer from his mug over the wooden surface. Pepper growls from beside my chair. "We don't want your *pirate filth* dirtying this establishment." The man grabs the front of my tunic.

"Let. Me. Go," I growl, letting loose the reins on my inner drake as my nails sharpen into claws.

"Or what? You'll take off with my girl, steal my treasure, and hide away in the ocean with your band of misfits?" he scoffs, swaying on his feet before taking a swig of his beer and spitting it at my feet.

I stand, grabbing the man by the front of his stained and torn jacket and hauling him up until his feet are dangling off the floor. "I said, let me go," I growl, the tips of my canines protruding past my upper lip. Flashbacks of pirates attacking father's ship momentarily blind me as red fills the edge of my vision. The smell of warm wet urine rents the air and my lips twist as I stare at the dark stain spreading across his breeches. "I think it's time for you to leave." I walk him to the door and throw him out. He lands with a thud on the ground, looking around blindly in the bright light.

"You'll... You'll pay for this! Sea curse you! May she take everything you love, you abominable creature!" he screeches before scrambling in the dirt, turning and stumbling away.

"Jokes on you. She already has."

I close my eyes and my chest constricts before I inhale. Casting my vision up, everyone on the street has stopped to stare. I turn on my heel and head back. The tavern is quiet as I return inside. I can feel all their eyes on my back as I take my seat.

"Two pints and some roasted meat," I call to the bar before pulling out a handful of coins and dumping them on the table, far more than enough to cover what I ordered.

I couldn't get back to sea soon enough.

It did not take us long before we arrived in front of a large glass paned shop. A small bell chimes as I push open the door, and I'm immediately met with the musky smell of leather.

"Ah, if it isn't Gavin Conway Lockheed," a wizened old voice says from behind the large wooden counter. "And what does this old lady have the pleasure of your company for?" She pulls out three large rawhide strips from her pocket and tosses them to Pepper.

"Hello, Cornelia." I bow sweepingly low. "You are looking as lovely as ever."

"Oh please," she scoffs.

"How quickly do you think you could make me a new pair of boots?" I sheepishly hold up the remnant scraps.

Her lips purse as she places her wizened hands on her hips, staring me down. "Has no one taught you manners, boy? What happened to, how are you, Cornelia? No, it's always business with you, Lockheed. That's what I get for saving your ass almost two hundred years ago!"

I lower my gaze, trying to hide the smile that's blooming on my lips. Cornelia is, in fact, the reason I'm still breathing. She was the one that tended her hand to me when the Gods had forgotten about Gavin Lockheed. When they had gazed upon three pirate ships ambushing my family's vessel returning with a shipment of Shadowvalian jewels, and had done nothing to stop them. When my mother had tied me onto a plank of wood, tears streaming down her cheeks, and thrown me into the open water as the ship was swallowed by the flames.

"Follow the stars, Gavin. Move your legs as fast as you can, reach shore. Live, my boy." And that's what I had done. I miraculously washed up on these shores without a scrap to my name, only grief in my heart and pain in my legs.

I blink, casting away the haunting images of my past. From the corner of my eye, I see Cornelia turning and beginning to up the shelves of handmade leather satchels.

"Cornelia, you know I–"

"Don't you *Cornelia* me, Gavin Lockheed. I may be old, but you're as hard as an oyster, cloistering yourself on that ship alone. You're going to work yourself to death. You can't even hold a civil conversation anymore." Worry laces her tone, making me feel guilty for not having visited in over a year.

Crossing my arms over my chest, I try to lighten the mood. "That's absurd, I am not going to work myself–" but I stop as she turns and raises an eyebrow at me. Rolling my eyes, I sigh and go to her side, Pepper at my heels.

"Cornelia, sweetest shell in the sea, how have the days been treating you?"

"Humph, now don't sass me." She leans down and gives each of Pepper's three heads a good pat. "Now tell me, what happened to your boots?"

The sound of heavy steps on the cobblestones outside the shop draws my attention to the front window where a royal guard precedes a gaggle of petticoats and parasols.

The most beautiful woman I have ever seen links arms with one of the other ladies as she doubles over with laughter, making my heart clench. Seven seas. Her eyes, cerulean blue like the unbroken horizon of the sea, stand out from her honey kissed skin. Without even realizing, I take one step closer to the window.

"Ah, I see the queen and her retinue are out enjoying the seaside. Any catch your fancy, Gavin?" Cornelia breaks the spell I'm under and winks at me.

I turn in her direction again and regain my composure. "I don't have time for dalliances. The sea is the only mistress I need." But I cannot help the tug that forces me to glimpse one more time out of the window. I watch her cascade of dark waves undulate with each step. She glances over her shoulder for a split second before the guards following their group block my view.

"Mhmm," she replies. "You can return for your new boots in two weeks."

"Two weeks?" I exclaim, turning around but she has already disappeared behind the curtain separating the shop from the back.

"Aye, and you won't get there a moment sooner if you know what's good for you. You don't rush destiny." She shouts at me, and I know there's nothing else I can say to change her mind.

Pepper pushes their wet noses against the back of my hand.

"Fine," I say with a huff as I turn toward the door. "We might as well head back to the ship and see if Rowan has made any progress."

CHAPTER THREE

Evie

"I tire. You are free to go," Queen Rose says, stifling a yawn as she gracefully drapes herself on a lounge in the sitting room. "Enjoy the evening as you see fit."

I curtsy before glancing around the room at the four other young ladies attending.

"Thank ye, Your Majesty," I reply with only the barest trace of my lilt before turning to take my leave. The royal summer house is nearly three times the size of my home. I race back to my room and throw open the balcony doors, inhaling the deep, rich ocean breeze. Using my powers has drained me somewhat, but I can still feel its exhilarating force coursing through me. Sometimes, I wish I could shed my restraints, become one with the flame. Feel powerful.

Vessels, both big and small, dot the ocean's horizon, making me wonder which remote corner of the world they are sailing toward.

"Evangeline!" a sweet feminine voice squeals from the door. "Grab your parasol and come! We are taking the carriage back to town to shop for new ribbons and hatpins."

A grin tugs at the corners of my lips as I turn and see the other ladies standing outside my chamber doors. "Only if we can stop at the patisserie shop and order more chocolate bon-bons."

"Those were to die for!" Ellie fakes a swoon, her golden waves swinging around her frame. She gives a shy smile in thank you for helping her regain control of her powers. Ellie had profusely apologized to the queen, but I had not failed to notice the slight tremor in her hand that followed her failed performance.

"That wasn't the only delicious thing in town," Charlotte says with a wink. "Did you guys get an eyeful of the—"

"Hush!" I whisper and roll my eyes, making the four of them fall into a fit of giggles and flushed cheeks. "We will be in Verdigris Falls all summer. There is no need to fall over the first pretty thing ye set yer eyes on."

"Not all of us can be as lucky as you and be engaged to a duke," Annalise says with a pout.

I turn away, hiding my face as my gut clenches.

"Have you met him yet?" Ellie asks sweetly.

"Is he handsome?"

"What is he like?"

"How large are his lands?"

"Do you think he could be your fated mate?"

"Oh, to find one's mate so young," Charlotte sighs dreamily.

Their questions come flooding as I busy myself by grabbing my parasol and changing into my boots. I plaster a well-practiced smile on my face before turning to face them.

"I'm sure all of you will find your fated mate or be blessed with an equally adventitious marriage, as the goddess wishes," Rinetta, my maid, says as she enters the room, arms laden with fresh linens and a new gown for tomorrow's dinner. I remind myself to thank her later for sparing me the torture of answering the girls' questions.

"As the goddess blesses," we all reply in unison, bowing our heads.

"Now, run along girls, I hear you've been allowed the afternoon to yourself. Don't squander it, stick together and stay with the guards. Verdigris Falls is a beautiful city, but even beauty can hide dark intent." She points to the sun through the open balcony already making its way past midday before shooing us out.

"I don't think I can eat another bite," I say, gently wiping the crumbs from my lips with a napkin. "Those are the most delicious scones I have tasted in my entire life."

We sit at a small round table at our favorite café. The salty tang of the sea mixes with the warm aroma of freshly baked bread, filling the air.

"Well, it's a good thing because I think we've missed dinner," Annalise replies matter-of-factly. "Not that I'm complaining. This was the first afternoon I've enjoyed myself in months. My mother hired extra tutors for language, etiquette, dancing, and the arts after learning the queen had chosen our family for one of her ladies-in-waiting. She said, if I wanted a suitable marriage, I had to prove my worth. What is painting worth to a husband? Although I can think of a way or two in which we could use paint for fun..."

We all fall into giggles over our tea. Charlotte fans herself to mask the red hue gracing her cheeks, and Ellie laughs so much she eventually snorts, making us laugh even more. Annalise has a smug expression on her face, happy she was able to lighten the mood after our eventful afternoon.

These women have become something akin to sisters to me. Despite our differences—of which there are many—we share the fact that our lives are bound by duty. That the freedom and privilege we have is a simple illusion, and that eventually, when the time comes, we have to do as we are told.

"It looks like there is still some daylight left before we have to return to the summerhouse. Anywhere else ye'd like to go?" I ask.

"Can we stop by that quaint little jewelry shop, The Pearl? It's near the leather shop right outside the docks. We strolled past it this morning. They had the most beautiful trinkets in the window," Ellie asks as she pushes up from the table.

"That sounds wonderful. I'd love to stop and see if I can order my maid a new pair of boots while we're in town." After many attempts at giving Rinetta some money to replace her old and worn boots—which she refused—I had decided I was going to get her some, nonetheless.

The golden rays of the sun glint off the surface of the waves as they crash against the rocky shore. A breeze ruffles my hair and I glance up to see storm clouds gathering on the horizon.

"Ladies, it looks like a storm is blowing in. We should turn around and head back for the summer house. It's a good hour's drive in the carriage," one of the queen's two guards says, gesturing to the sky.

"Don't be silly," Annalise says as she parades down the street to the shops. "Those clouds are miles away. We aren't likely to see a storm for hours."

I glance again toward the clouds that have taken on an ominous purple tinge. "Perhaps he is right. We can always come visit the sh–"

"Evangeline. Live a little. Where is your sense of adventure? Plus, we're nearly there!" Charlotte points before she rushes up, entwining arms with Annalise.

Ellie looks at me with a shrug and I can't help but sigh and smile. "Alright, get going, I'll be right next door."

I watch as she runs off, guards in tow, when I feel a sudden warm tug in my core. I turn toward it and fail to notice the horse frothing at his mouth, charging in my direction with a runaway cart.

CHAPTER FOUR

Gavin

I throw my body protectively over hers as Pepper jumps before the horse, grabbing its reins in one of its massive jaws and pulling it to a stop inches from us. "Good boy," I pant as I brush the hair away from the girl's face, my fingers coming away sticky with blood.

"What is going on?" A male shouts. I glance up and see a guard rush out of a shop followed by a group of females, before returning my attention to the girl before me.

"Wake up. Oh, by the goddess, please wake up." My drake form paces inside like a caged beast wanting to be free. Wanting to curl around and protect this female before us.

"Evangeline!" One of the females cries as she lands on the ground beside me.

Evangeline.

"What happened? Guards, we need a healer!" she shouts, recoiling as she sees the blood.

"The palace healer is back at the queen's estate," the male says quietly. "That's an hour away."

"I have a healer," I growl out, my fingers wrapping protectively around her frame as I hoist her into my arms. "My ship is down the dock. She's losing too much blood to wait." The two other girls wail, glancing between their friend on the ground and the female in my arms.

"Perhaps the town has a healer that can come and see her." The other guard says, warily looking me up and down. "We wouldn't want to inconvenience you... sir."

"The town's healer is out delivering a babe. I saw her off not even an hour ago. She won't return for some time," the wise old voice of Cornelia speaks from behind the crowd that has gathered around us. "Let Gavin take the girl off to be looked at. Don't let his tough exterior fool you. He is a well-respected gentleman and loyal to a fault to the crown. He will have her healed up and ready to serve the queen. It is you who should hurry if you wish to make it back to the queen's estate. Those storm clouds are rolling in fast." She lifts a wooden cane to the sky and I follow it, dread coiling in my stomach as lightning flashes across the darkening sky.

"Rowan!" I bellow as I rush across the gangplank, holding the female to my chest. "Where is Rowan?"

"Captain, sir." Callen rushes over from where he's securing the rigging. "She's downstairs cataloging inventory. Who is this?"

I brush past him, wind whipping my hair and clothes as I head down the stairs and kick open the door to my cabin. "Go get Rowan and bring her here. Now." I gently lay her on the bed. "Evangeline?" I ask as I brush away the matted hair from her face. My heart leaps as her eyelids flutter.

"What is going on, Gavin?" Rowan's voice calls from the door, arms laden with her wooden healing chest. "There is a nasty storm brewing that'll be on us at any moment." As if to emphasize her statement, a gust of wind blows out the candles as it slams the door shut.

"Damn it!" I let the leash loose on my beast, feeling my wings snap out from the slits in my shirt. My fingers sharpen into claws, my canines elongate as I reach out to ignite the hearth and every candle. "Heal her," I demand as I turn my head toward her.

My mind is racing and I struggle to make sense of what just happened.

"Who is she?" Rowan wastes no time pushing up her sleeves and placing the chest on the bed. "And move your giant draken ass to the side, for ocean's sake."

A low growl escapes me as I move to the other side of my bed, giving Rowan room to work. Pepper leaps into the foot of the bed, laying its three massive heads across her legs. "She's one of the queen's ladies-in-waiting."

Rowan lifts an eyebrow, her hands pausing above the female's scalp as she meets my eyes. "And pray tell, Captain, why is one of the queen's ladies on our ship, bleeding all over your sheets and not being attended by the royal healer?"

Evangeline lets out a low moan, her eyebrows furrowing. My throat tightens in response and I am on the verge of losing my gods-damned mind. "Shhh, you will be alright," I whisper as I gently fold her hand into mine, stroking the back with my thumb. "A horse nearly ran her over. She tripped and fell, cracking her head on the stones."

"That much I can discern by her injuries. My question is: why is she here?" I watch in awe as Rowan's magic guides the liquid to run from the bottle all the way through Evangeline's hair like tiny glowing rivulets.

"She–" I pause, body tensing. I watch her face relax as Rowan's magic slowly heals her injuries.

Why is she here? My racing heartbeat echoes in my ears. I could have let them take her to the royal healer. Gods, I could have even flown her there, but everything happened so quickly. The brief meeting of our eyes, the cruel twist of fate that put her in danger's way, and then the panic rising like the tide—the instinct to save and protect this woman rushing over me.

There is one word lingering on my lips. One that explains this desperation I feel.

The word tastes familiar, like the salt-laden air wrapping around me on deck, like the golden hue of the sun emerging from the horizon. It's sweet and right, but it also holds an ancient power to it. One that terrifies me. I look at Evangeline's fragile frame, and wonder, why her? But no matter how much I try to rationalize this feeling, the word is still there. Waiting for me to embrace it. I gently squeeze Evangeline's hand and hope destiny knows what she's doing.

Mine.

"Gavin?" Rowan's whisper snaps me back to reality, her brows furrowed.

"I think she's my fated mate," I let out, shocking even myself.

"Oh!" Her eyes widen, but she immediately gets back to work, pushing Pepper out of the way to examine Evangeline's ankle. "Are you sure?"

"I've never felt like this in the one hundred and seventy years I've been alive." A loud boom of thunder echoes, rattling the walls, and we both glance up.

"Perhaps the goddess is looking favorably upon you. It's not likely this storm will let up for quite a few days," Rowan says as she gently pries off Evangeline's boots. She secures her ankle in a wrap before standing, wiping her hands on her coat.

"If this is her way of doing favors, it's an odd way of showing it," I grumble. "Will she be alright?"

"Yes, nothing appears to be broken. She's likely to have a nasty headache when she wakes up. Have her drink..." She rummages in her chest and pulls out another corked bottle and a small silver thimble. "One dose of this. It should dull the pain and keep the nausea at bay. I'll have Chef start some stew and bread."

"Thank you." I lift my head but only catch her coattails as the door clicks softly behind her, leaving me alone with a woman I don't know but to whom my heart already belongs. My mate.

CHAPTER FIVE

Evie

I wake to a dull throbbing pain in my head, nestled in a bundle of warm blankets that gently sways around me. The sound of torrential rain makes me want to turn to the other side and fall back to sleep. Surely, the queen won't want to go on her morning stroll in this weather. But as I crack open my eyes, I'm greeted by the panting faces of three enormous dogs.

No, it's one dog with three heads.

ONE DOG WITH THREE HEADS?!

I clean my eyes with a groan, lifting a hand to my forehead. I must be hallucinating. The last thing I remember is a male with alluring eyes like molten gold, then tripping as I tried to avoid a horse attempting to take my life and, finally, the world going dark.

A cold wet nose nudges my cheek and I chance another peek, noting that there is indeed a giant three-headed beast laying in the bed with me. I push to sit, taking in deep breaths as I will the room to stop spinning. My body tenses when I notice the man slouched in a large wooden chair next to the bed.

It's him.

His head lolls on his chest, and I cannot help but be drawn to the dark stubble that lines his chiseled jawline and his auburn hair pulled back at the nape of his neck. My heart speeds in my chest as I take in his full figure.

Stunning.

The word catches me by surprise and I immediately pull the bedsheet higher up to cover my chest. The fog that clouds my mind clears and I realize, to my displeasure, that this is not my bed, I don't know who this male is and—based on the room's swaying and the lack of comforts—I am on a ship.

Before I panic further, the wooden door to the room opens and in walks a tall, lithe female with pink skin, silvery blonde pixie cut hair and pointed ears. "Ah, good. You're awake. How are you feeling?" She sets the tray laden with food on the table before turning to me.

"I–" Suddenly, the room sways to the side and my stomach lurches. "To be honest with ye, I don't feel so good. Where am I?"

She rushes to my side and places a hand on my shoulder. A wave of cool sensation emanates from her hand. "Breathe in through your nose and then slowly release. Drink this." She lets go and reaches to the nightstand to fill a silver thimble with a dark violet liquid.

"What is it? And who even are ye?" Wrinkling my nose, I sniff at the liquid before glancing between this girl, the dog, and the male still asleep.

"Do you want to feel better or not? My name is Rowan. Gavin here rescued you after your little accident. He brought you aboard our ship so I could heal you." She frowns, glancing at the male then out the door toward the stairs. "It was either this or traveling an hour to the palace to get you to the royal healer, and let me tell you, you'd have not reached the destination alive, not after all that blood loss."

I sip at the concoction, pleasantly surprised at the saccharine taste. If the ladies and the guards had allowed this man to take me, they must have trusted him. "I'm Evangeline. Thank ye." I look between Rowan and Gavin. "Does the queen know where I am?"

"Yes, Evangeline," Gavin says, voice gruff with sleep. "Everyone knows you're aboard the Quartz Thorn. Rowan has been with me for years. She's the best healer I know. I trust her with my life." It feels as if time has stopped. My head snaps toward the sound of his voice. It has a familiar and comforting lull to it, the kind of voice that makes me want to close my eyes and listen to it narrate stories full of adventure.

Gavin sits up straight and I notice his body tense, his chest expands as if he is holding his breath in anticipation—for what, I am not sure. I feel my magic well inside me and the prickling sensation on my fingertips snaps me back to reality where I realize, with utter embarrassment, that I have been staring at this man.

"Oh! Good. Yes, excellent." My cheeks are flushed and all I want is to disappear under the blankets and pretend I do not exist. "I am feeling much better, thank ye." I nod to Rowan, who is leaning against the door frame with her arms crossed, studying me as if I were a puzzle.

Avoiding her scrutinizing gaze, I start plaiting the mess that is my hair.

"Well, now that you're awake and feeling better, let's get you cleaned up." She grabs a wash basin, cloth and bar of soap from the nearby table and makes quick work cleaning the dried blood crusted to my forehead and hair before handing me a brush.

"We could have a tub filled-" Gavin cuts in.

"The poor girl just woke up and is probably starving," Rowan says, with a last inspection of my head and face. "That'll have to do for now. Later, we can fill up a tub for you."

"Thank ye," I say as I brush the tangled knots from my tender scalp and finish plaiting my hair.

"Right, if you need me, I'll be back down doing inventory." Rowan scoffs and leaves the room.

"How long do ye think the storm will last?" I ask Gavin after a moment and gather all my courage to meet his eyes, causing a fluttering sensation in the pit of my core. Without a satin string to tie my braided hair, I leave it hanging over my shoulder.

"We are still docked in Verdigris Falls, but this storm isn't likely to clear up for travel for at least a few days," he says as he leans forward, bracing himself on his thighs.

I cast my eyes down, cheeks heating. "I'm sorry to be a burden on ye. If there is any way I can repay ye–"

Calloused hands gently grip my chin, tilting it up until my face is only inches away from his. He runs his thumb trailing along my bottom lip causing my breath to catch. "Evangeline, you owe no debt to me."

My head tilts to the side as I focus on the hues of bronze in this stranger's eyes. His touch keeps me anchored to him and I wonder if he's ever going to let go. I also wonder what his full lips...

"It's, ehm..." I withdraw and try to put some distance between us. "It's Lady Evangeline, actually." What is wrong with me? The lessons on manners and propriety come back to me with a vengeance. I square my shoulders and keep my chin high, even though I am certain Mother would faint on the spot if she knew I am alone with a man, and in his bedchamber, no less.

But my restraint lasts only a moment when I notice the massive membranous wings folded behind him. Maybe I am indeed hallucinating.

"Oh my..." I tentatively reach out a hand to caress its edge, but Gavin's firm grip clamps around my wrist, bringing it in between us.

"I'm so sorry," I blurt, covering my mouth with my free hand. "I hope I did nae offend ye, I've never seen a Draken shifter before."

His body relaxes. A shy smile tugs at the corner of his lips and he releases my wrist. "No, you did not offend me. My wings are just—sensitive."

Another crash of thunder booms and I shiver, clamping my eyes shut. I take one deep breath and hold it for a second. Then, I slowly breathe out through my mouth.

When I open my eyes again, Gavin's brows are furrowed. He shifts and his weight causes the bed to sink, and I'm suddenly aware of how massive he is compared to my petite size.

"Not fond of storms, I assume?" He reaches to his hair and lets it fall loose on his shoulders. Stretching his hand in my direction, he offers me a string of leather and points to my braid.

"No, not really. Especially not on a swinging ship." I take the string and my fingers gently brush his, setting the embers within me alight once more. Securing the end of my braid, I add, "Logically, I know it's just sound but it terrifies me as much as watching the storms fascinates me."

"Storms are a thing of beauty," he says in a low voice. "But they can be equally violent and destructive. It's the reason we're in port for more than a few days." Just then, a warm wet tongue rasps against my cheek and I can't help but giggle.

"Thank ye." I turn my head to the dog. "I don't think we've been properly introduced."

"This mangy beast," Gavin says as he pushes off the bed, "is Pepper. He's the most annoying creature you've ever met with a voracious appetite. But he's loyal. I've had him since he was a pup."

He gives each of the giant three heads a pat. Pepper's tail beats at the bed wildly, their tongues lolling, drool dripping.

"Oh! Yer shirt!" I gasp when I notice the blood stains marring the white linen.

"It's just a little blood. Nothing a good scrub won't get out." He glances down at the sleeves, and before I can take another breath, he reaches for the hem of his tunic and pulls it over his head.

My lips part and my eyes widen as I take in the thick ropey muscles that flex and bunch with his movements.

I should cover my eyes. Avert my gaze to something other than his broad shoulders and chest, other than the fine dusting of bronze colored hair that disappears behind his trousers. But by the gods, my gaze only dips lower and a strange curling sensation hits my stomach, pulsing deep in the core between my legs.

He grabs a clean shirt from a nearby drawer before returning to face me and I watch as his nostrils flare. A shimmer of magic makes a pattern of scales form along the column of his throat. He takes a step toward me, his gaze so intent on my mouth that it is like a caress. My heart begins to beat wildly in my chest.

"Are you afraid, my Lady?" The way he draws out each syllable is my undoing.

"No," I whisper back. I can feel my magic sing under my skin as he moves closer, begging to be freed.

"What do you want, Evangeline?" He drops his tunic forgotten on the foot of the bed as he braces his right hand on the mattress beside me.

"I want–" I swallow, contemplating the questions. It was the question I had wished my parents had asked me before marrying me off to Lord Charles. The question I had asked myself on so many sleepless nights when I felt suffocated by the growing pressure of marriage and the expectations bestowed on me as the only heir to my father's fortune.

I want to live for myself, as naïve as that sounds. Experience things without having to worry about how it'll affect my reputation in polite society. I wish to not have to conform, to not have to perform. And most of all, I want to share life with someone who yearns for the same freedom I yearn for. But no matter how strongly I desire all of this, I cannot have it, and this stranger in front of me won't be able to solve my conundrum either.

So I shyly smile at him, lifting a hand and letting flame dance along my fingertips. "I want to touch the scales on yer neck."

"You cannot burn me," he says as he presses my hand to his neck with his free hand. I marvel at the velvety soft feel of them blending seamlessly into the human skin beside it. Each overlapping scale has an iridescent shimmer of blue. If only I was a painter talented enough to capture their essence. What a masterpiece that would be.

"And what, my Lady, is your second wish?" His eyebrows lift as a grin tugs at the corner of his lips.

I can't help but chuckle at his infectious smile. "I want something to eat."

CHAPTER SIX

Gavin

"How long was I out for?"

"About eight hours. It's nearly midnight. So it doesn't surprise me that you're hungry." I smile, offering her a hand. "Come, let's head down to the galley and see what the chef has prepared. Do you feel up to walking?"

"I'm starving!" She exclaims. I place her hand into mine and swing her legs over the side of the bed. She winces as her feet touch the wooden floor and my whole body freezes. "I'm okay," she says.

"No, your ankle is sprained." Despite her cry of protest, I swing her into my arms.

"Put me down. This is highly inappropriate. I am not a feeble wee lass needing to be carried." Her lips purse as she stares me down.

"This is my ship, pearl, and as the Captain, I make the rules. Come, Pepper," I command, throwing the door open and heading down the stairs. The boat rocks as another loud clap of thunder reverberates through the ship. In my arms, Evangeline slams her eyes closed and shivers. "The Quartz Thorn has been through a lot worse. You're safe with me."

Pepper lets out a bark of approval, pushing between my legs and leading the way to where the savory scent of stew wafts up from below. Evangeline buries her head against my chest as thunder rumbles throughout the hall.

"You need to count," I say tentatively, taking one stair at a time.

"Pardon?" She raises her head in surprise, one eyebrow arched.

"Count the number of seconds that pass between a flash of lightning and the crack of thunder that follows." Absent-mindedly, I rub soothing circles where my hand cradles her back. "Divide the number by five and it'll tell you how far you are from the eye of the storm." My inner drake growls in contentment as the tension in her body relaxes.

"Is that some sailor's wisdom?" she asks, her cerulean eyes full of curiosity.

"More like a captain's wisdom," I say with a charming smile, and to my surprise, I continue. "Well, if I must be honest, my mother taught me the counting trick when I was a boy. It helped me fall asleep during our long journeys on my father's ship. It's one of the few memories I have left of her." My heart constricts at the mention of my mother. I have not talked about her in over a hundred years.

"Well, thank ye for sharing this memory with me, Captain. I will make sure to start counting next time lightning hits the sky." Her fingers brush the back of my neck and it takes every bit of strength I have to not run back to my chambers and hide this wonderful creature from the rest of the world.

But before I lose my lucidity and before more memories come back knocking at my door, we reach the bottom landing and I push open the door to the galley.

"Captain!" A cheerful voice rings out as Chef walks out from the swinging doors of the kitchen, arms burdened with a large tray of mugs. "And finally a beautiful face to brighten up the room. Who is this sweet song bird?" His bright white smile stands out from his brilliant green skin, jet black hair peppered with gray pulled into a knot at the top of his head. I set Evangeline down in the nearest chair and can't help but brush a stray lock of hair from her face.

"This, Chef, is—" I start.

"Lady Evangeline Rose Gramont," she beams, holding out a hand. "But ye may call me Evie."

"Charmed, mademoiselle. What a pleasure to meet such a beautiful lady as yourself. You may call me Chef, everyone else does."

I narrow my eyes at her in challenge. I, the captain of this bloody ship, have to stick with Lady, but Chef can get away with Evie.

She tilts her head to the side, an eyebrow raised. "Chef? Do ye have a given name?"

"Ah yes," he says, throwing her another dazzling smile. "But only my mother calls me by it. Now, what can I prepare for you?" Chef bows low and, as if reading my mind, Evangeline looks at me with a snarky smile on her beautiful face whilst the man bestows a chaste kiss to the back of her hand. Something deep inside me slips and a low possessive growl escapes me, making half the heads of my crew turn in my direction.

"Gavin," Rowan calls, a note of warning in her tone. I meet her gaze and clear my throat before pulling up a chair next to Evangeline, an arm draped along the back of the wooden backrest. With a glare, the rest of the crew returns to their conversations.

"Oh! Surprise me!" She clasps her hands in front of her. Chef grins, his dark eyes dancing with mischief.

"You just said his three favorite words," Rowan says and Chef gives out a chuckle.

"I may not look it, but I love food." He rubs at his flat stomach. "The kitchen is a palace and I'm the king."

"Don't go over inflating your already swollen ego, old lizard man," I say as I punch him lightly in the shoulder. "I don't need you leaving me to petition for a spot in the royal kitchens. Who would keep poor Pepper content? He'd be a wild beast without your coddling." Pepper lifts his three heads off the floor, tongue lolling and dripping into a puddle on the waxed wood floor. His tail whacks at the wood, rivaling the thunder that booms around us.

"Are ye a dragon shifter, too?" Evie asks.

"Nah, I hail from the island of Cyprian. My family are lizard shifters, but I love the sea, and after meeting Gavin, I couldn't pass up the opportunity to explore this ragged world. I've been with him for nearly fifty years," Chef says. "Well, I best get back to cooking before a riot starts."

Rowan pulls her seat over to our table and reaches out, gently prodding the back of Evie's scalp. "Are you feeling better?"

"Yes, thank ye," Evie replies meekly before turning toward me. "I need to send word to the Summer Palace. I need them to send a carriage as soon as the storm is over."

My chest constricts at her words. I lean back in my chair and rub a hand over the rough stubble on my chin.

"Already tired of us, my lady? Do you have some prince charming to run off to before midnight?"

Evie turns her wide eyes toward me, a tinge of pink blossoming in her cheeks. She clenches one of her fists, sadness clouding her eyes. But a split second later, as if slipping a mask back on, she doubles over in laughter and scoffs. "I am no princess, Captain. But as ye correctly stated, I am a lady, one of Queen Rose's ladies-in-waiting to be correct, and as such, I have duties I must respect." She casts her eyes wistfully up the stairs, where the pounding of rain can be heard through the dense wood.

"*Must*," I repeat, dragging the word.

"Pardon?" Her head tilts and there it is, her polite smile—the one she's probably been taught to put on to please everyone around her—falters.

"You said you have duties you *must* respect. That does not sound like something you *want* to do." Evangeline narrows her eyes, studying me, and I wink almost imperceptibly.

"Well, whether you want or must, it does not change the fact that you're stuck with us for now, and there is plenty to keep you occupied," Rowan says as she downs her drink, forcing me to look away from Evie. "Gavin's a wizard when it comes to blowing glass. Have you ever seen it?"

"It's cheating because he's a fire drake," one of the crew calls jovially from a nearby table.

"Glass blowing?" Evie cocks her head at Rowan.

"Yes, it's one of the many things we trade in. Down the coast of Khalifi, they sell powdered metal oxides and minerals mined from their mountains that we can use to color the glass." She nods.

"How fascinating!" Evie clasps her hands together, her face lighting up. "I would love to see how it's done. But is it safe inside a wood ship?" She raises an eyebrow as she casts a glance around the room.

"Oh pearl, you're on a ship with a variety of magical creatures who travel abroad to numerous faraway lands. Fire is the least dangerous thing this ship has been warded against. But don't let a little bit of danger scare you off, my lady." I smile.

CHAPTER SEVEN

Evie

Rowan opens the heavy wooden door before us, and the pungent, acrid scent of smoke immediately assaults my nostrils. As we step inside, my eyes are drawn to a large pit in the center of the room, its surface covered in dark soot stains. The walls are lined with barrels of varying shapes and sizes, emanating an earthy aroma. Above them, an array of rods, pipes, shears, and an assortment of unfamiliar tools are mounted on the walls. I am carefully placed in a worn-out chair by Gavin, who rubs his hands together, creating a faint, rhythmic sound. Annoyed, I purse my lips together and assert, "I can walk, ye know."

"You need to stay off your feet until your ankle heals completely, I'm afraid I can't disobey Rowan's orders." Gavin turns his head toward her.

"I think yer worrying too much, and not putting enough faith in my healing ability," she replies as she starts to pop off a few of the lids, pouring their sand-like substance into smaller bowls on a tray. "Why don't you stop dilly dallying and get the fire going, Captain?" She set the tray down on a small wooden table at her side before grabbing an armful of wood from a pile and tossing it in the pit.

"It's not that I have little faith in your healing ability. But I am conscious of the fact that the queen will have our heads on spikes if poor Evangeline were to injure herself further under our care."

His skin begins to ripple as scales slowly materialize and his canines lengthen. Gavin's eyes take on an unearthly golden glow as he concentrates on the wood. The colorful illustrations from one of my history books, The Compendium of Shifter Metamorphosis, come back to me. As a young girl, I used to trace over those illustrations endlessly, learning all the names and details of every shifter group in existence in preparation for the grand adventures I'd embark on once I was older. Unicorn shifters were my favorites: smart, loyal, and ethereally beautiful. But as I watch the magnificent sight that is Gavin in his draken form, the little girl in me smiles and wonders if maybe we have a new favorite type of shifter.

Rowan turns and grins at me before helping me to my feet. "She's stronger than you give her credit for. Just be careful of the heat."

Flame licks along Gavin's hands, tendrils of blue, white and purple consuming the wood. He moves his arms in a rhythm, drawing the flames into an orb of white heat and I can feel his magic pulsing, drawing me into its dance. Without even realizing, I'm at the edge of the pit, my hand reaching out to caress the flame.

"Feed the flame with your magic," Gavin whispers, and I withdraw. Confusion etches his face.

"N-no. I cannot possibly do that." I clench my fists and attempt to return to the wooden chair, carefully balancing on my hurting ankle. Before I can turn, Gavin grabs my wrist with his left hand now free of flames.

My magic sings under my skin, begging to be let free, but I can't. Ladies have no need for magic, because with magic comes lack of control and a lady must be in control at all times if she wants to be the matriarch of her house. This is how it has always been, and how it will always be.

Powers not utilized and practiced are wasted.

The queen's words interrupt the lies I've been forced to take as truths and I meet Gavin's scrutinizing gaze.

"A fire elemental scared of her own fire?" He baits me with a snarky grin, but curiosity etches every word. The room is quiet and all of a sudden feels way too claustrophobic. Rowan's eyes bore through my back.

"I am not afraid of my fire, if ye must know," I spit, freeing my wrist from his grip and taking a step back, but my heart pounds in my chest. The scent of warm amber and cinnamon bark envelops me, intoxicating and comforting at the same time.

"You won't mind helping with the fire, then. All that carrying you around has tired me." My already hot cheeks from standing so close to the fire flush even further.

"I didn't ask ye to carry me around, Captain. And I have no obligation to prove myself to ye." With a flick of a hand, I conjure a fire butterfly that disappears in the roaring pit. I raise my chin high but my fingertips burn as if they too touched the core of the pit. The air seems to crackle with electricity, charged with the intensity of our connection.

"Come on now, pearl." His voice almost a purr. "That's just a little trick. Show me what you've really got in there." His gaze holds mine, unwavering.

Driven by spite, and something I am not able to name, I step closer, feeling the magnetic pull between us grow stronger. Resting my hand on his, I close my eyes, will my body to relax, and let my powers loose.

The embers within me turn into a roaring inferno but instead of suppressing it, I guide it. The naturality with which the magic inside me follows my commands is exhilarating. I tilt my head to the side and a moan of contentment escapes me, reminding me of what is happening.

When I open my eyes, Gavin's lips are parted, his eyes wide in awe. A tingling sensation spreads from the tips of my fingers and surges through me, awakening every nerve ending. I glance down and see flames of the most beautiful orange dance on my body, and where mine and Gavin's fire meet, the flames have a hypnotizing shade of purple—reminiscent of raw quartz.

Slowly, Gavin moves his hand so our palms touch and I feel as if a burden has been lifted off my chest. As our flames waltz in unison, a tug, deep and ancient, pulls me closer to this man who I have only just met. "Evie," he whispers.

A voice clears behind me, and I startle.

"Believe me, I am just as embarrassed to have witnessed whatever is going on between you two, but if you don't stop, you are going to burn all the wood up—and gods forbid the whole bloody ship—before you've even made anything," Rowan says, holding up a bowl of glass chunks and a rod toward Gavin.

It takes us a second to break the contact and put some distance between us.

My legs shake at the realization of what just happened. I have let my restraints loose and I have not lost control. The world has not ended in flames.

Limiting the flow of power coursing through me, I suppress the flames and try to focus on what Rowan is explaining. "First, you have to melt the glass. Then you gather the molten glass from the furnace on one end of the blowpipe."

"But won't it harden?" I ask as I take the offered pipe and Gavin pours the glass into a crucible set on top of the pit on a special rack.

"If it hardens, you heat it back up in the flames."

"Now, the fun begins. We're going to make a simple decorated goblet. We have a whole collection of them that we're planning on selling at the next dock; Rowan can show you later."

My heart clenches at the cruel reminder that this is but an idyllic pocket in time. When the storm is over, I will leave and so will he. As I am lost in thought, Gavin moves behind me, his towering figure embracing me and guiding my hands. I am aware of every point of contact between his body and mine as we collect the molten glass from the crucible onto the end of the steel pipe. We then dip it into the colored powder and back into the flames.

The warm glow of the flames casts dancing shadows on the walls of the room. The crackling sound of the fire intermingles with the soft hissing of the molten glass. The air carries a faint scent of burning wood and a hint of something sweet, like caramelized sugar. Gavin encourages me to send tendrils of my fire magic, stoking the heat as it softens the glass. We repeat this process and then move it over to another table set against the wall where he helps me shape it into a round orb.

As Gavin guides my hands, his touch sends a shiver down my spine, igniting a warmth within me. Every dip of the steel pipe into the colored powder is deliberate, the vibrant hues sticking to the glass like tiny particles of magic. Gavin's fire magic dances around, its tendrils stoking the heat and caressing the glass, transforming it into a malleable masterpiece.

"Now, for the magic." He takes the pipe from my hands, lifting it up to his mouth and puffing a small amount of air as the glass slowly expands to a bubble.

With each breath, the glass expands, fueled by the gentle force of Gavin's exhalation. His touch lingers on the glass orb, leaving a trail of warmth in its wake. I am captivated by the transformation—mesmerized by the interplay of silver, cerulean, and green, swirling together in a captivating dance. I can't help but marvel at the beauty before me, the way the light catches the shimmering surface, creating a mesmerizing display of colors. It's as if the glass itself holds a secret, a hidden enchantment waiting to be discovered.

"It's gorgeous," I say in awe as I watch him take the glass off the end of the tube with his bare hands, then use a pair of the tools to stretch the mouth of the goblet open like a blooming flower.

"And that is why the crew says he cheats," Rowan says, breaking the spell. "Any of the rest of us touch molten glass and we'd burn our hands off."

As the healer takes over the pit, starting a new project, the workshop hums with creativity and camaraderie. The molten glass continues to dance, its ever-changing form a testament to the skill and magic that resides within this space. And amidst it all, I realize that maybe, this is the adventure I was waiting for. Maybe Gavin is the one who can set me free.

CHAPTER EIGHT

Evie

"What time do ye suppose it is?" I yawn as we make our way up the stairs from dinner. "I don't think I can eat for a week after that delicious meal. I've never had such a tender roast."

Gavin pulls a watch from his pocket and flips it open. Silver entwined dragons are engraved on the inner surface. "Looks like it's nearly midnight."

"We should best get to bed, then." He pushes open the door to his study, his hand a gentle firmness on my back guiding me. "Where can I sleep?"

I look around the wooden panel room. The walls are adorned with intricate carvings, depicting sea monsters battling on the ocean waves. The floor-to-ceiling shelves are filled with weathered books, nautical charts, and trinkets. A soft glow emanates from the brass lanterns hanging from the ceiling, casting dancing shadows across the room. The large wooden desk sits proudly in one corner, stacked with neatly organized papers and a quill pen. My attention is momentarily captured by the massive bed, still rumpled from my previous slumber.

"You can have my bed for the remainder of your stay... my lady," he says as he turns and lights the lamp on the table.

"Oh I couldn't possibly impede, again. Ye won't get any sleep sitting upright in the chair. Perhaps ye have an extra cot in the crew's quarters?" Even as I say it, my stomach turns at the thought of sharing the room with so many people.

"You won't be sleeping with the crew," he growls. "None of them are to go near you or lay a hand on you."

"Ye don't trust yer crew with me safety?" I turn defiantly and face him with my hands on my hips.

"No, that's not..." he pauses and rakes a hand through his hair. "You deserve the best. Not a cot with the crew, not one of the hammocks hanging in this ship. You deserve the fine silk we import from the island of Scintillante which, coincidentally, is on my bed right now." He points to the rich red sheets, and I remember the exquisite feel of them when I had first woken up. "I will sleep on my armchair next to you, if that pleases you."

Heat floods my cheeks as the memory of him leaning over me on the bed asking me for wishes comes back. I glance down at my soot stained dress and chemise.

"I suppose that will do. Could I possibly borrow something to sleep in so that I can wash my gown? I would hate to soil yer bed." I gesture toward my skirts.

He rummages in a large chest of drawers before tossing me a white, cotton long-sleeved shirt. "Will this do? I'm afraid I don't entertain female guests often."

"Yes, thank ye." I clench the shirt before me and in a whisper, I add, "and thank ye for earlier, for pushing me with my power. I am usually not allowed to indulge in my magic, it's not *proper*."

Gavin takes a step in my direction. His hair still hangs loose over his shoulders, and I wonder what it would feel like to rake my hand though the strands.

"You are most welcome, my lady, and if I may, fuck propriety." There is a second of silence lingering between us before we start laughing—so much so that my cheeks eventually start hurting. But when the giggles subside and the awkwardness returns, Gavin comes even closer.

"When the flames embraced you," he whispers. "I have never seen anything more beautiful in my entire life. Trust that I have not known you long, but... it changed you. It was like witnessing a flower bloom right in front of my eyes. That fire is part of you." The sincerity in his words makes my eyes burn. For so long, I was made to fear this power—to suppress it—only for this stranger to barge into my life and prove the opposite. And the funniest thing of it all is that I believe *him*.

Panicking at the intensity etched on his face, I look at the shirt still in my hands. "Uhm can ye, give me some privacy to change?"

"Oh, yes." He turns around and I watch the muscles of his back flex as the fabric pulls taunt over his back. I quickly slip out of my gown and chemise before slipping the shirt over my head. It falls below my knees and I have to roll the sleeves up at the wrist. I inhale deeply, the scent of cedar and cinnamon clinging to the fabric.

A loud banging pounds on the door causes me to jump.

"What is it?" Gavin calls out.

"It's Pepper," Rowan's voice calls out from behind the door. "He's missing."

Gavin marches to the door and yanks it open. "What do you mean he's missing?"

She leans against the frame panting and dripping water everywhere before pointing down the hall. "One of the crew went to check the rigging and a peel of thunder boomed out, and he said Pepper ran between his feet. We searched everywhere on deck but we can't find him."

"Damnit." Gavin yanks on his boots and turns to me. He freezes for an instant, his eyes taking the image of me in his shirt, and then continues. "Stay here, I have to find that beast." He heads down the hall.

I stand debating before impulsively heading after him.

The rain pelts against my face, mingling with the salty spray of the sea. The boat lurches and groans, its wooden planks straining against the relentless waves. The howling wind drowns out my shouts, carrying them into the night. Lightning illuminates the swirling mist, revealing glimpses of towering waves that threaten to swallow us whole. The air is heavy with the scent of damp earth and brine, a potent reminder of the treacherous waters surrounding us, even in dock. Fear grips my heart, each beat echoing in my chest as adrenaline courses through my veins. The urgency to find Gavin and the dog intensifies, driving me forward despite the chaos around me.

"Pepper!" I cry out as the storm rages on. Using my index and thumb, I whistle, hoping it'll catch Pepper's attention enough to signal his whereabouts. The dark clouds swirl above me, releasing torrents of rain that pelt my face like icy needles. Thunder booms in the distance, echoing through the vast emptiness of the open sea. The salty air fills my nostrils, a mixture of brine and damp wood. The ship groans and creaks under the relentless assault of the wind, its timbers straining against the fury of the storm. I whistle again and again. The deck is slick with rainwater, making every step treacherous and uncertain. I struggle to maintain my balance as the ship pitches and rolls beneath me. If this is how much the ship moved at anchor in dock, I don't want to imagine being caught in a storm at sea.

Crawling along the waterlogged planks, I reach a bundle of boxes. They are haphazardly secured, their contents hidden beneath layers of soaked tarp. The wind whips the material around. I grip the wet surface, feeling the rough texture against my fingertips. The wind howls around me, drowning out any semblance of sound. The rain continues to cascade down, soaking me to the bone. Every movement is a battle against the elements, a constant struggle for control in a world consumed by chaos.

In the silence following the boom of thunder, I hear a small whimper. With renewed purpose, I gather my strength and push myself back onto my feet. Taking a deep breath, I whistle one last time and brace myself against the relentless wind as I make my way around the boxes when I see Pepper, huddled on the ground, his massive heads buried under his paws. I breathe a sigh of relief as I reach him and bury my hands in his fur whispering reassuring words.

"Gavin!" I yell as I tug at Pepper's collar toward the door, but he digs his paws into the wood, shaking. "Gavin!" I feel for the bond I had felt when our magic danced together and tug, pouring all my thoughts and feelings into it, praying it will work.

Moments later, I see him marching toward us in the flashes of lightning. My heart races as he embraces me. The warmth of his touch contrasts with the coldness of the rain-soaked clothes clinging to my body. Every drop of water that cascades from my trembling form carries away the tension and fear that had consumed me just moments ago.

Inside the ship, the harsh flashes of lightning that had illuminated the stormy night are replaced by the soft glow of the candlelight. As I glance down at the dog, I see my same relief glimmering in his eyes.

CHAPTER NINE

Gavin

"What were you thinking?" I ask as I set Pepper down and grab her by the shoulders. "I told you to stay here."

"Ye cannot tell me what to do, and I couldn't simply sit and do nothing," Evangeline retorts with anger, and I can see glimpses of fire in her eyes.

"Do you have no concern for your own safety? What if a gale wind picked you up and threw you over the railing?" My heart clenches at the thought of the ocean consuming her.

"My safety is none of your concern, Captain. And if you had waited and listened for one second, I would have told you that I have spent a summer learning how to train my father's hunting dogs and that I could have helped."

"Well, how was I supposed to know that, *Lady Evangeline?*—"

"—Do not patronize me!"

"Do you even know how terrified I was when Rowan told me you went on deck?" She crosses her arms over her chest, stretching the fabric of my shirt over her breasts, but I stay focused. "You have tormented me since I saw you outside of the leather shop this morning, and when I could not see you on deck, I was ready to empty the ocean drop by drop to find you."

Evangeline stares at me. "That's a reckless and impossible endeavor."

"I am aware of that and yet, not even the Gods would have been able to stop me."

She blinks, meeting my gaze, raindrops falling from her lashes. I follow as they trail down her cheek, continuing down her neck to her collarbone. My white linen shirt is soaked and clings to her skin, the pink of her nipples standing as defiant as her temper. Soaking wet in my shirt, she resembles a sea goddess, a siren sent directly from the depths of the ocean to torment me.

Mine.

My wings flair out curving protectively around her slight frame as our bodies clash together. I slide a hand behind her head and crush her lips to mine. She melts under my touch, her body melding against mine. I tease her lips with the tip of my tongue, begging for entrance as I let my other hand trail slow lazy circles down her back. She moans, sliding her hands hesitantly up my chest and around my neck, almost sending me over the edge. My inner beast roars to claim her, mark her and it takes all my strength to rein him back. I didn't want to scare her.

"My lady," I pant, resting my forehead against hers. Everywhere her body touches mine, I burn hotter than I ever have.

Evangeline shakes her head. "Evangeline," she says breathlessly. "I want ye to call me by my name"

My lips crush into hers again and wander off to explore the soft skin of her neck. I repeat her name in between kisses and it sounds like a blessing. Evangeline tilts her head back, abandoning herself at my mercy.

"Please, Gavin," she whispers, and my name on her lips is my undoing. My claws shred the back of the shirt clinging to her body, careful not to mar her silken skin. I step back, admiring the candlelight flicking over her sweet pale figure before sweeping her into my arms and carrying her to the bed.

The mattress dips under my weight as I stretch out beside her and run a hand along the curve of her hip.

"There's no jewel more beautiful than you..." Heat flushes across her cheeks as I grab her chin and press a soft kiss to her lips. "Who'd have thought it would take a storm to bring clarity to what I was missing in my life?" I brush her hair away to expose one pert nipple and she freezes under me making me pause. "What's wrong?"

"I'm..." Emotions flicker across her face before she wraps her arms across her chest and closes her eyes. "I've never–"

"You've never been with another before?" I nuzzle at her cheek and curl a wing protectively around us, cocooning us closer. "Evangeline, look at me."

She hesitantly lifts her gaze, eyes hungry with desire but also something akin to fear.

"We don't have to do anything you're not ready for, but I want you to know, I will worship every inch of you." I trace a finger down the side of her face before running my thumb along her bottom lip. She is so fucking beautiful and it is taking all my will power to rein in my beast from making her truly mine in my bed with the goddess forsaken storm raging around us.

But then, like lightning across the sky, she lights up with newfound certainty. She darts her tongue out, flicking it against the pad of my thumb and I close my eyes as I shiver in pleasure.

"Gavin," she whispers, running her fingers across the stubble of growth on my cheeks. "So many choices have been taken from me but tonight, this, I want it to be my choice and I want it to be ye." I hold still as she lifts her hand to caress the soft flesh of my wing above us, letting her set the pace. Her wide eyes are set on mine and there's an echo of awkwardness again.

"But I don't know how... eh, what... to do," she whispers, and before the panic in her voice can grow, I kiss her.

"Will you let me guide you? You don't have to do anything you don't want to. And I will stop whenever you want me to, pearl." Her breathing relaxes and she nods.

"Yes," she whispers and the word rings true.

Tentatively, she explores the plain of my chest, going lower and lower at an excruciating pace. When she nears the waistband of my britches, she looks up at me and I nod encouragingly. She lets a finger trace the painful bulge in my britches begging to be freed, her eyebrows lifting as she continues along its length. "Oh–"

I chuckle and reposition myself to straddle above her. "I won't hurt you, Evangeline. Plus that's not all the fun, pearl. I told you I will worship you, if you'll let me." There's anticipation shining through her. I gently grab her wrists and pin them above her head before I lose my control.

I trace my hands over the soft skin of her abdomen as I lean forward and trail kisses between her soft pert small breasts. She arches under me, letting out a moan of pleasure.

"I want you." I take in a deep inhale of her, lavender and vanilla, and feel my canines slightly elongate, throbbing to mark her as mine. I let the tips gently scrape across one nipple, soothing it with a kiss as she writhes below me. My hand drifts lower, drawing slow deliberate circles as it makes its way to the valley created by her thighs.

"It's alright," I whisper and she slowly unclenches her thighs allowing me to stroke her nub. My lips capture the gasp that follows hungrily.

"Oh, Gavin," she whimpers, her legs clamping together again as her hips buck up to meet my hand.

"Spread your legs, my pearl," I demand. I slip one finger through her wetness and nip gently at her neck. Moving, I slide my leg between hers to keep her open. I slip a finger inside and my britches tighten painfully as she moans my name. I pull back before plunging in deeper, letting my thumb trace circles around her sensitive nub. "Evie, you're...so..." I growl, claiming her mouth, our tongues dancing together as I slowly increase my pace. I slide in a second finger, plunging deep into her molten core. With a cry, she arches against me and I feel her pulsating around my fingers before collapsing onto the bed panting. "Goddess, you're the most beautiful creature I've ever seen."

"May I touch ye?" she whimpers. Her eyes are a stormy cerulean as she darts her tongue out to moisten her lips. She writhes beneath me, pulling at her restrained arms.

"In time, my pearl. I am not done yet." I release the grip on her wrists and reposition myself between her legs. I stretch out my wings behind me. Her eyes widen and her nipples tighten from the air current created by the movement. I slide my hands under her hips and gently blow warm air across her sensitive mound, watching as she trembles.

"Gavin, what are ye doing to me–" she gasps, threading her fingers through my hair as I lick her. Her hips writhe as I begin to worship her. My fingers dig into the soft flesh of her thighs as I devour her until she collapses trembling against the sheets.

"Sweet as caramel," I growl against sweet flesh before trailing kisses up her body and I claim her mouth. She smiles sleepily as I pull back, admiring her face. "Sleep, my pearl, I will keep you safe from the storm."

CHAPTER TEN

Evie

A knock at the door jars my attention. I pull the sheets to cover my breasts and peer around the room, looking for my discarded soiled clothes, but all I see is what remains of Gavin's tunic shredded on the floor. My cheeks flood with heat as I call out, "Gavin? Is that ye?"

"Good morning, Evangeline." Rowan bustles in the room, carrying a bundle of wrapped parcels and laying them on the bed at my feet. "I'm afraid your clothes are still wet from washing. Gavin had me run into town and fetch what I could. Can't have you seeing the Queen improperly dressed." She gives me a wry smile and winks.

Untying the bundle, I gasp as the paper falls away to reveal three garments. A chemise of viridian blue silk that flows through my fingers like the ocean water, a cream one, a fur lined cloak with matching gloves and kid skinned boots. "I can't possibly accept this. Where is Gavin?"

"He's off to fetch a carriage to take you back to the Queen's estate now that the storm has subsided." She rummages through the wood drawers until she pulls out a silver brush and comb set. "Come now, I'm not a ladies maid but can help you tame that wild mess you have going once you are dressed."

"Thank ye," I say, nodding in appreciation as thoughts begin to reel through my head.

"I will say I'll be sorry to see you go. I haven't seen the captain so jolly since he laid eyes on you. But I'm sure you miss the queen and life at the palace."

I pull the chemise over my head and step out of bed as she helps me pull on the overgarments and tighten the corset. She grabs the brush and gestures to me onto the chair before working on my tangled locks.

"I–" My throat suddenly feels tight and hot tears prick at the corner of my eyes. I don't want to go.

How am I supposed to marry Lord Charles after this, after Gavin? Even if I confess that I am no longer suitable for marriage, I would then have to suffer through all the shaming polite society will put me under for lying with a commoner. Not to mention the embarrassment I would cause my family. Their only heir is a whore, how pathetic. And what will the other ladies say? The queen would be ashamed to hear that this is how I repaid her hospitality, by jumping into a stranger's bed.

What do you want, Evangeline?

Gavin's words come back to me and hit me like a blow. You, I want to say. I want him, and I want for us to stay on this ship—no matter how naïve that sounds. I want to use my magic freely, have it cursing on my skin. I want him to count with me every time there's a storm. And I want to argue with Gavin, over and over, so he can then kiss it all away in forgiveness, because...

Because he is my mate.

My lips part at the obvious realization, and for the second time in less than two days, I feel like another burden has been lifted off my shoulder. But how do I tell him that I am to be wed?

"Sorry miss, the wind and the salt water from the sea spray last night locked in knots somewhat wildly." Rowan interrupts my thoughts. "After my first year on the ship, I learned I either had to chop my hair short or always keep it pulled back. I'm almost done." She makes quick work braiding my long hair into a crown around my head before pulling out a wooden box from her pocket and pinning it in place with pearl and spun glass hair pins.

I gasp at my image in the small mirror she hands me as I gently prod the masterpiece. "It's beautiful, Rowan. But..."

"No buts, the captain insisted. Oh! And this." She pulls a strand of white pearls from the box and drapes it around my neck. "Now let's get your stockings and boots on and head up to the deck. I daresay the carriage should be here any moment."

But my legs struggle to move.

The sun shines bright as we make our way across the walkway to the dock. My gaze is instantly drawn to him. He is standing in front of one of the royal carriages, arms crossed, deep in conversation with the driver. My heart leaps with joy and I take off running toward them, Rowan following closely on my heels.

"Gavin!" I cry out as I reach the two men. I place a hand on my chest and take a moment to catch my breath as they turn to face me. My lips turn down as Gavin turns to me, his face a mask of stone.

"Tha–" I begin.

"Good, I'm glad to see you're ready for the journey, my lady," he says. "The queen is eager for your return and has sent a carriage."

"But, Gavin." My brows wrinkle as I stare from him and the proffered carriage door opened by the footman.

"Actually," the driver pipes up in a wise crackly voice as he looks between Gavin and myself. The queen has requested both your presence. We must not keep her ladyship waiting."

I climb in and take a seat on the plush velvet seats. The carriage rocks as Gavin steps in and takes a seat opposite of me, his wings barely fitting through the door. He crosses his arms over his massive chest, leans back his head and closes his eyes.

The next hour passes in near silence. I grip the cushion beneath me each time he deflects conversation or answers with a grunt.

"Why are ye being so cold? Did I do something wrong?" I reach out and nudge his knee with my gloved hand. He opens his golden eyes, and with a sigh, rakes a hand through his hair.

"No, Evangeline. You could never do anything wrong."

"Then, why are ye acting this way?" My chest constricts when he refuses to meet my gaze.

"You're a lady with your hand promised to a duke," he says, turning to look out the window. "And I'm promised to the sea. We come from two different worlds."

The carriage comes to an abrupt stop and I nearly tumble into his lap. The door opens and we are both ushered into the queen's waiting room, who joins us moments later. She walks over to her chair and sits with the grace of a dancer before gesturing to us. "Please, sit. I'm so glad to see you in good health, Lady Evangeline."

"Thank ye, yer majesty." I curtsy to the queen before taking a seat in the lounge across the table from her. "It is good to be back in yer company, although I was in good care on the Quartz Thorn with Captain Lockheed and his healer." I tuck my hands politely in my lap.

"Ah yes, your great rescuer. You'll have to tell me all about it. The girls were in such a tizzy when they came back. The stories have grown more outlandish by the hour with all of them stuck inside the last couple of days with that dreadful storm." The queen claps her hands before turning to face Gavin, who continues to stand near the door. "Now, for the matter of favor for rescuing one of my ladies in waiting."

"It is not necessary, Your Grace. It was merely the right time and place, thank the goddess. I just wanted to ensure her safety back into your care. If I may request my leave? My staff is nearly finished with the repairs to my ship, and then we must sail off," Gavin says and I whip around in my chair, chest constricting. He keeps his gaze steady on the queen and I turn away, cheeks flushing.

"Nonsense," says Queen Rose as she claps her hands. A page boy runs to her side. "I'll be throwing a ball in one week's time to celebrate the summer equinox. I'd be delighted to have you as a guest of honor for rescuing Evangeline. I expect to see you there. You may take your leave now." She raises one eyebrow at him.

"As you wish," he says and bows deep at the waist. His gaze meets mine and I feel that incessant tug deep in my core burning like the hottest flame, before he turns around and walks out the door.

"Fetch us some tea," she says and I turn around to face her. She waves off the page boy before turning back to me. "Now, I may not be old and wise, but I know that look. What is it you wish to ask me?"

"I—" Heat blooms across my cheeks as a hundred scenarios play through my mind of our time together. I clench my gloved hands tightly in my lap at the scent of burning fabric.

"Evangeline, the look on your face is the same I saw a dozen of times when I first met the king." She pats my hands and a sense of calm washes over me. She pushes to her feet and moves over to the edge of the room where an easel sits facing away from us. "I know of your engagement to the duke."

"Of course, Yer Majesty. It is my duty and honor to accept the betrothal from ye and the king. My father and mother—"

"Come here, Evangeline." At her words, I look up and meet her kind gaze before moving to her side. "The duke and you would make an honorable marriage and he would treat you kindly. He would provide you with anything your needs required and you would serve the kingdom as his duchess." My stomach turns sour and I bite the inside of my cheek to maintain my temper.

"Do you know what I'm best known for?" she asks as she runs a hand over a soft cotton cloth covering the canvas

I shake my head, wondering what she's getting at.

"Since I was a young child, I was blessed by the goddess not only with the power to control wind, but also with the ability to see visions of the future through my art." She grabs the edge of the canvas, gripping tightly until her knuckles turn white. With a sigh, she turns to me and smiles softly. "Knowing the future is a heavy burden, Evangeline, but as the ruler of Shadowvale, it has benefits to all of the kingdom."

"It can't be easy to carry such responsibility, especially as a child," I say.

"Worry not. At this point in life, it has become somewhat of an old friend. Now to the matter at hand. The duke is coming to the ball next week. Would you petition me to break off the engagement?"

"I couldn't poss–" My eyes widen and I take a step back.

"Nothing is impossible, Evangeline. I wish to break your engagement, for the goddess has blessed me with a vision. It's a selfish wish, but I think it would benefit us both. If I break the engagement, you'll be free to marry the draken shifter, but you'll become a permanent member of my queen's ladies and my confidant. This mating will bring you the ultimate joy and the deepest sorrow. Knowing this, would you still accept?"

"Queen Rose." My throat tightens, tears pricking at the corner of my eyes. "What if he won't have me? What if he won't leave the sea?"

She smiles, a sad twinkle in her eye before pulling off the cloth with a flourish. I gasp as before me is a painting of a young boy with the strong, handsome Gramont facial structure but with Gavin's coloring carrying a fair haired boy of the same age with bright blue eyes in a bloody torn tunic.

"I grant your wish because one day, your child will save mine, and in turn, they will save the kingdom." She fondly traces a finger over the smooth paint of the boy's figure as a tear slips down her cheek.

CHAPTER ELEVEN

Gavin

"What am I doing here?" I mumble as I step out of the carriage. The soft glow of lanterns guides my way as I approach the grand entrance. Melodic strains of a string quartet drift through the night. The air is thick with the heady fragrance of blooming jasmine and heather mingling with the salty breeze that whispers secrets from the nearby sea.

As I make my way up the path, the gravel beneath my boots crunches, echoing my restless thoughts. With each step, the imposing estate looms larger, its windows aglow with the warm flicker of candlelight and dancing fire. I loosen the constricting tie around my neck, seeking a momentary release. I was not made for court life, not like she was. But I had to see her one last time.

With a deep sigh, I glance up, sending a prayer to the goddess. Above, the night sky is a canvas of deep violet, adorned with a celestial tapestry of twinkling stars.

"Sir!" A voice cries out and I turn as a messenger runs across the ground. "The ball is this way. If you continue that way, you'll only find the sea." He bows, then points to the large glass doors that were flung open. I stare down and find I've walked knee deep into the rolling heather.

"Thank you," I say gruffly with a nod before heading back toward the estate.

Through the open doors, women in long colorful dresses dance with males in well-cut suits. Onlookers stand at the edge of the room, clapping, laughing, and sipping on flutes of bubbling liquid. I push up the billowing cream sleeves of my tunic and frown at my best black trousers. I stand out like a piece of coal in a sea of gems.

And then I feel her, my Evangeline.

She stands gracefully in a flowing gown the color of the sea on a stormy day, hugging her slender figure and flaring out at her hips. The sheer sleeves dance and ripple in the breeze, as they brush against her skin. Her hair, a cascade of dark curls, is partially pulled back, allowing the soft tendrils to caress her shoulders. As I gaze at her, my eyes are drawn to the strand of pearls I gifted her, resting gently against her bosom.

Mine.

A deep growl resonates inside me, causing a few ladies to titter and turn in my direction but I ignore them as I make my way across the room, to her. The dance changes and I switch direction to avoid careening into the dancers. When I look up, she is gone. I study the room until I spot her again, her arm looped through that of a tall male with short blond hair in a tailored navy blue suit. He stands with a male who knows wealth. He must be the duke the town was in talks about all week. The duke who is engaged to one of the queen's ladies maids.

Evangeline frees her arm from his and curtsies low to the queen. The duke follows suit with a deep bow and a chaste kiss to the royal crest on the queen's proffered hand. At this distance, over the music and chatting, I can't discern their conversation but my gut clenches. Claws and teeth lengthen as the duke smiles charmingly at the queen. With a nod, he reaches over and lays a hand to the middle of Evangeline's back and leads her to the dance floor.

I storm from the room, running blindly into the night. *Fool,* I tell myself. Always so mesmerized by the illusion of loyalty when not even the sea herself grants you that. She'd sooner drown her sailors than let them discover her secrets. Love is no better.

CHAPTER TWELVE

Evie

Twisting my hands together, I rock onto my toes and look around the room. Where is he? He promised the queen he would come. Had he changed his mind? Had something else befallen him?

"Evangeline?" A deep voice calls out to my side, breaking my spiraling thoughts. I turn and paste a smile to my face.

"Yes?" A tall, handsome blond male bows low beside me. "Your portrait does not do your beauty justice, my lady. Are you looking for someone? A lover, perhaps?" He raises an eyebrow.

I sigh and comb my fingers through my hair. "A... friend. But it looks like they've changed their minds on coming." He takes two flutes of sparkling drinks from a passing servant and I accept one gracefully.

"Well, that's a shame. Don't let this ruin your evening. The queen's balls always have the most curious of details. I hear this one has a special guest in attendance that rescued one of her ladies?"

I nearly choke, having a coughing fit as I turn to the stranger. "Do I know ye?" But his attention is drawn over my shoulder. I turn, but all I see is Annalise and Charlotte chatting and pointing at the dancers.

"It's *her*," he whispers. I feel the earth slightly tremble beneath my feet.

"Are ye alright?" Turning, I place a hand on his forearm and I can feel his magic pulsing off him in waves.

"Evangeline, I must speak to the queen." He offers me his arm. "Would you please accompany me?"

"Of course." I hand off my glass to a passing attendant and loop my arm through his. We make our way weaving through the crowd of onlookers until we get to the queen's side.

"Evangeline," she says as she smiles warmly. "I see you've made the acquaintance of Duke Charles."

I curtsy before Queen Rose as Charles bows beside me. "Yes, yer majesty. We were admiring the marvelous job ye've done on such short notice."

"Well, life is short. You must enjoy every moment the goddess grants you," she says.

"Queen Rosaline," the duke says as he bows low and bestows a chaste kiss to the signet ring on the queen's proffered hand. "It is my pleasure to be in your company once again, but I'm afraid I have a request of you."

"Speak your request, you have done much for the kingdom," she replies, leaning back in her seat.

The duke places a hand on the small of my back making me tense up.

"I'd like to request to call off the engagement," he says.

"Pardon?" I turn to face him as my stomach somersaults.

"I am so sorry, Evangeline. Destiny has dealt me a card I cannot ignore, not even in the face of duty. I gave my word that our marriage would be the solution in uniting our people but goddess forgive me, keeping my word will only ruin both our lives. I have spent over three hundred years waiting for my true life's mate, and she is here, Evangeline. I cannot be the husband you deserve."

The duke's words have rendered me speechless, and I am torn between laughing at the utter perfection this is, or crying because for me and my mate, it might be too late. The queen hums softly as she smiles between the two of us. "Well that does put me in quite a position." She drums her fingers together and my chest constricts.

Beside me, I feel the duke tremble as the ground beneath us rumbles. Such a powerful earth elemental would be a benefit to the kingdom, indeed.

"Well, who am I to get in the way of something as ancient and true as a mating bond?" She claps her hands and waves us away.

"Go, dance and be merry. Bring me this girl and, if she consents, I shall make the announcement at the end of the ball."

I let loose a breath and follow the duke as he turns me around to the dance floor, and that's when I see him. Gavin storms out of the room, lords and ladies move out of the way as his wings flare behind him and he disappears into the night. My chest constricts and I step to follow him but I'm swept into the duke's arms as the musicians begin to play a lively waltz.

"Evangeline, I am so sorry," he says as we move in time to the music. "When I first stepped into the room, I felt this internal tug deep inside of me and I knew she was here. I know how important marriage is to—"

"Charles," I interrupt him and move us off the dance floor. "I am very happy for ye, I truly am, but I have to go right this moment."

"Lady Evangeline, you don't have to hide—"

"For the Goddess, Charles! This has nothing to do with ye. Go and introduce yerself to yer mate and let me run after *mine*." As if I've slapped him in the face, the duke's hands drop to his sides. I watch his gaze focus somewhere behind me. I follow it to where Annalise is dancing with a little boy; she's the picture of pure joy.

"Make haste, duke. Destiny does not wait around." I give him a final pat of encouragement before I storm off.

Annalise and Charles are going to be phenomenal together. As an Earth Elemental, he would be the perfect ground for her wild spirit and magic as an Energy Elemental. But whilst opposites do undoubtedly attract, a dragon burns brighter with his flame.

I clutch the side of the queen's carriage as we ramble along the dirt road back to town. I catch glimpses of the ocean, sparkling in the sunrise through the rolling hills dotted with boats leaving and coming into the harbor.

A loud crunch makes us stop abruptly a few hundred feet from the edge of town. I throw open the door, jumping down.

"What is the matter? Why have we stopped?" I ask as I peer at the carriage twisting my hands together.

"I'm sorry, Lady Evangeline, but I'm afraid one of the wheels has broken on the road. The repair is going to take a while but we can go into town and fetch another to come get you," the driver says sheepishly as he begins to unhook one of the horses.

I look between the horse and the road ahead of me that ends at the docks.

"I don't have time. Give me the horse!" I demand and move to help loosen his bindings from the carriage.

"But your ladyship," he protests but continues working the leather straps. "We don't have a proper saddle."

"Time is of the essence," I say as I yank the last strap free. "I grew up riding horses bareback."

Using the carriage as I leaver, I hoist myself upon the creature's back as the driver hands me the reins.

"Goddess speed," he says but his words are lost to the wind as I spurn the horse forward, praying I'm not too late.

The land rushes by, the wind whistling and whipping my hair behind me as I race toward the dock. My chest tightens, tears prick my eyes as the wind catches the mast and the massive wooden ship begins to pull away right as we hit the edge of the dock. I slow the horse to a stop, sliding off his back and falling to my knees. He skitters to the side before finding a patch of grass and lowering his head to graze.

"No," my voice cracks as my vision blurs. The Quartz Thorn is nowhere to be seen.

CHAPTER THIRTEEN

Evie

I bury my head in my hands, my body trembling with each wracking sob that escapes me. Alone at the docks, I wait for the queen's carriage to arrive to take me back to the estate. Back to my monotonous life. I had escaped the clutches of marriage but at the cost of true love—how ironic. A wave of physical pain washes over me, causing my chest to tighten until I can hardly breathe. The town and ocean around me blurs. It feels as if my very essence is being torn apart, like a storm raging within my soul, leaving me feeling raw. It is only fitting that my pain echoes the very storm that brought me the greatest joy.

Dogs bark in the distance followed by the sound of the waves lapping against the pier. I hiccup and brush the strands of hair out of my face but pause as my fingers touch the pearls on my neck. I unlatch the string and clench them in my fist until it hurts.

"Pull yerself together, Evie," I whisper but before I can stand, I am knocked to the ground by a beast and my vision is blocked by three massive slobbering heads.

"Pepper?" I push myself up on my arms bewildered. "Pepper, what are ye doing here? Where is Gavin?"

"Pepper!" A familiar male voice calls. I turn and catch sight of Gavin sprinting down the street. Our eyes lock, and he increases his pace until he reaches my side, dropping to his knees. He grabs me by the shoulder looking me over. "Evangeline! What are you doing here? Why are you on the ground? Why aren't you at the queen's estate? Are you hurt? Pepper, you roguish beast."

"Gavin," I whisper, new tears threatening to spill. "I thought ye had left. I saw ye at the ball but ye left and–Yer ship!" I turn and face the ocean, where the large ship has pulled further out to sea.

"My ship?" He chuckles and points further down the pier. "She's docked way down the ways. We moved her down the pier after the storm to help with some of the other smaller ships this week."

"Oh," I say and nibble at my bottom lip. "Then, why did ye leave the ball without a word?"

A mask of stone flashes over his face before he tucks a stray hair behind my ear and helps me up. "Evangeline, I am just a captain who cannot keep his feet on the ground. I was not joking when I told you, you deserve better. You are engaged to the duke. It's an advantageous union, one I am sure you are proud of and I wish you nothing but happiness, but don't ask me to witness it and pretend it does not kill me."

"Gavin, no. I *was* engaged to the duke but–" I start.

"What do you mean you were engaged? I saw you with the duke and the que—."

"Why can ye pig headed, stubborn males not be quiet for one moment and listen to me?" I pull out of his grasp and stomp my foot as I point a finger at his chest. "I want ye. I've wanted ye from the very first moment. With ye... I feel whole."

"But the engagement?" He frowns and crosses his arms over his chest. Pepper whines at our feet pawing at my skirts.

"The engagement was called off. The Queen agreed to it before the ball but then Destiny added her own twist and the duke met his true mate." He stiffens at the word *mate* and I hope it's because he too can feel that relentless tug between us too. I put my hands on my hips and pout. "Ye also owe me one more wish."

"Pray do tell, what is your wish, Evangeline?"

"I want to stay with ye, my mate." Tears glisten and my throat tightens as I stare up at him. Gavin's strong embrace engulfs me, his lips meet mine in a passionate kiss. As he twirls me around, the world blurs, the rush of excitement filling the air. With a tender touch, he sets me down, my heart still racing from the exhilarating moment.

"You don't even have to ask," he growls before stealing my breath with another kiss.

"There is just one little requirement," I say. "The queen has appointed me as a permanent member of her queen's ladies which would require me to travel with her."

"Oh, my pearl," he whispers, pressing his forehead against mine. "I will be yours, body and soul, until my dying breath. I love you."

"Even more than the sea?" I raise an eyebrow, waiting on bated breath.

"Even more than the sea," he repeats before sweeping me off my feet and heading to his ship. "It's about time I settle down, and Rowan is more than ready to take over. But first, there's some unfinished business we need to tend to."

between my legs at the muscles that flexed and bunched under his thin shirt now on display.

"Careful, pearl," he growls, prowling closer to me.

I push myself up onto my elbow, darting a tongue out to moisten my lips as my gaze travels down his frame. Even in the candlelight, I can see how tight his britches are and how they glove his body leaving little to the imagination. Gavin eases onto the bed, towering over me with his wings flared.

The panic of not knowing what to do and what to expect starts taking over me and I avert my gaze. Suddenly self-conscious, I attempt to cover parts of myself, but Gavin notices and slows down. He takes my chin in his hand and angles my face in his direction. Staring into his golden eyes, it feels as if he is watching right through me.

"Nothing has changed," he says in a stern yet gentle voice. "I will stop if you want me to. And I want you to remember, that in this bed—and any other bed we'll share—the power will always be yours. I am but a faithful priest worshiping at your altar." I nod and take a deep breath.

When I don't feel my heart wanting to escape my chest, I rake a hand through his auburn hair and revel in the fact that it is as soft as I had imagined.

"Then start worshiping, Gavin Lockheed."

He pushes his mouth hard onto mine, making me moan. I explore his full lips, sucking, nibbling and teasing, before his tongue slides urgently into my mouth, showing me without words just how much he wants me as the low, aching wave builds, threatening to shatter me into a million tiny shards.

"Gavin," I moan, writhing underneath him. "I'm burning."

He smiles against my lips before trailing kisses down the column of my neck. A strange curling sensation hits my stomach. He runs his finger along the neckline of my gown, following the rapid rise and fall of my breasts. "Impatient little thing." He cups my breast and swipes a thumb across the center, running it in slow tight circles. "Evangeline, you are mine."

"I am yers," I whisper, arching into his touch as his hand travels down the length of my torso. I grind my hips against him, desperate for friction against the burning, flooding through my veins. "I need ye."

"You need me to do what?" He smirks, slowly pulling my skirt up. The feeling of soft silk sliding against my skin is sweet anguish, only further stoking the need growing inside me. I roll my hips again, eliciting a low growl from him.

"Take me as yer mate, yer wife. I don't want to spend another day without ye. Ye complete me in ways I never thought possible, but right now, yer absolutely torturing me," I pant.

Gavin smiles lovingly at me, tracing a claw tipped finger down my jaw before grabbing the front of my bodice and ripping the fabric in two. My exposed nipples pebble at the rush of air. "You are the most delectable creature I have ever seen," he says before dipping his head and licking at their perky tips. "I promise I'll be gentle, my pearl."

"If ye keep ruining my clothes, we will have to bring on a seamstress full time," I chuckle, running my fingers through his hair.

"Or I could just keep you to myself in our chambers, where you wouldn't need any clothes." His voice is a rumble against the sensitive flesh of my chest and I moan. "I will know every inch of your beautiful flesh." He pushes the torn fabric down my hips and slides a hand between my thighs.

My fingers wander down the planes of his muscled chest until I reach his waistband. I tentatively run my hand across the firm length of his arousal and abandon myself to what I hope is some innate instinct that will tell me what to do.

"You're making it hard," he growls against my ear.

"I can tell." I smile as I start to undo the buttons until he springs free from his confines. I marvel at it and the way running my hand down its length causes Gavin to tremble and makes his breath hitch. His firm caress against the pulsing ache between my thighs increases and I cry out as pleasure pulses through me.

"Fucking seas, Evangeline, you are so wet." I gasp as his fingers gently caress my wetness, nudging my thighs further apart.

"I need ye, Gavin." I wrap my hand around his smooth girth and stroke him. The irises of his eyes burn with a golden molten flame as he drops his forehead against mine and moans. I freeze, my fingers still tight around him. "Am I doing it right?"

He chuckles, then claims my lips in a kiss. "You can do nothing wrong, my pearl."

A thrill runs through me as I continue, watching his body tremble with every drag of my wrist.

"Evie," he moans, stopping his torturous caress to grab my wrist, halting my movement. "Do you know what that does to me?" His eyes flash as he stands off the bed and kicks his trousers the rest of the way off before climbing onto the bed between my legs. "If you keep that up, I can't promise I'll be gentle." His fingers bite deliciously into my thighs, his claws pressing into the skin as he spreads me wide. He hovers over me, gaze roving from my face to the pulsing heat now on full display.

"And if I don't want gentle? If I want to play with fire?" I taunt, my toes curling under his heated gaze. All the nervousness and awkwardness has disappeared. I feel bold and wanton, my magic singing in my veins and a need building inside begging for release.

"You are as wild as the sea herself. I would give you anything you want. We have all the time in the world, Evangeline, my love." Gavin releases my thighs bracing his hands on either side of my head as his thickness presses against my entrance. I see his canines elongate and after I nod in encouragement, he thrusts inside me with one smooth movement as he sinks his teeth in the crook of my neck.

I cry out at the sharp pain in my neck and core. Fiery hot electrical currents race from his bite and I lose hold on my magic. My hands are living flames as my nails dig into his back. He holds still as I pant, my body arching to accommodate his thickness filling me. He presses gentle kisses to the column of my neck whispering to me in a language I don't know.

"My pearl," he whispers, and I know it's a question.

"I am fine. More than fine. Keep going." He nips at my earlobe before pulling slowly in and out, each rock of his hips bringing him deeper, bringing our bodies closer. His massive wings hang around us like a powerful curtain. He moans my name as his rhythm increases, dropping his head against my shoulder. "I love you, Evangeline."

"And I love ye, Gavin." A pressure begins to build inside me and I writhe, nails scraping down his back as I lift my hips to meet his thrusts. He kisses me with fervor, our breaths mingling as he runs a hand through my hair, tightening his grip and pulling back my head to expose my throat. "More," I moan, and he increases his tempo. Magical tension fills the air, competing with the pressure building in my pelvis. "Gavin, I–" my words catch as he moves his other hand between our bodies stroking the delicate bundle of nerves.

"Burn, my sweet pearl. Let it consume you," he growls. I cry out, my body shattering into a million pieces as fire burns through my veins. He holds me until the last trembles ebb from my body.

"Gavin, that was–" he claims my words with a kiss before beginning to thrust once again, slowly building into harder thrusts. I moan, arching beneath him as his movements begin to build up another cresting inferno inside of me.

"Oh pearl, we're only just beginning." Trapped between the sheets and his hot, muscular body, every touch scorches my sensitive flush. "I want to claim you. I want to mark you as mine so no other will ever doubt who belongs to you."

"I am yers," I whisper and moan, closing my eyes as his hips continue to increase tempo, pushing me deep into the mattress. Gavin roars with one final deep thrust, his wings flaring behind him before leaning down and sinking his fangs into my shoulder. I am on fire, from the pulsing of his length buried deep inside me to the magic burning from his bite, but I don't care. I am happy. I am free.

of times. The only difference is that I won't have to worry about your ass." Rowan punches his shoulder, and he snaps his wings, frowning.

"Yes, but–"

"No buts Gavin. The queen has already left for the capital, and we are to meet her to go over the trade treaty Rowan is to propose." I smile sweetly to him. "Plus, we have to move into our new house in the capital. Rowan is ready. Say goodbye to the sea and come keep me warm on the journey." I wink, pushing up from the ground and turning to the carriage waiting patiently behind us. Pepper follows closely at my heels; he jumps on the front of the carriage and curls up on the floor next to the driver.

Gavin sighs and rakes a hand through his hair before pulling his new captain into a firm embrace before holding her an arm's length away.

"Go enjoy your wife, Gavin. If the two of you didn't manage to burn the Quartz Thorn down, I am sure she can withstand anything." Rowan backs up and gives him a cheerful wave before turning and heading up the gangplank. Gavin turns and climbs into the carriage, closing the door behind him.

"Hello there, husband," I tease.

"Come here, wife," he growls. He grabs me by the waist and I laugh as I fall into his lap.

"It's a long way to the capital," I muse, pressing my forehead to his.

He strokes my back in slow, tantalizing movements, the corners of his mouth turning up into a grin. "Oh, I think I know a way we can pass the time."

His hands slide up my skirts and settle me further into his lap until the evidence of his arousal pushes against my core. I gasp and playfully slap his chest. "Gavin! We are in a carriage, with the queen's guards only separated by wood paneling."

He growls, pulling my head down into a possessive kiss that leaves me breathless. "And you are my life. I want you and I will take you here and now, you wanton little fire witch, queen's guards be damned." He loosens his breeches and I gasp as he rips away my undergarments with his claws and slides me over him in one smooth motion.

"Ye beast," I gasp, my cheeks flushing as he spreads my thighs, lifting me up and down, building a rising friction.

"You like my draken side, don't deny it." He slams down my hips, and I cry out as waves of pleasure wash over my body.

"More," I pant into his neck, breathing in his deep scent of cedar and cinnamon.

"As my lady commands," he growls. My skin hums with electricity, molten heat building into a crescendo as Gavin picks up his pace. He roars and I feel him pulse inside me before I tip over the edge as waves of ecstasy consume my body. He holds me as I tremble in his arms until the last of my orgasm fades. He presses a gentle kiss to my brow and I nuzzle my head into the crook of his neck, letting the rocking of the cart lull me into a deep sleep as my draken wraps his wings around us both and whispers in my hair, "In the hottest fire, even a stone heart can burn."

Printed in Great Britain
by Amazon